Race Cars

Written by Jo Windsor

Rigby

In this book
you will see cars that
can go very fast.

You will see...

race cars

parachutes

helmets

Look at this race car!

A race car driver
races cars like this.
The cars can go very fast.

Race car drivers like to drive fast.
The fastest car wins the race.

A race car driver must be safe.

He wears clothes to keep him safe.

He wears a mask.
He wears a helmet.
He wears gloves on his hands.

The driver wears clothes to keep him safe. Why?

helmet

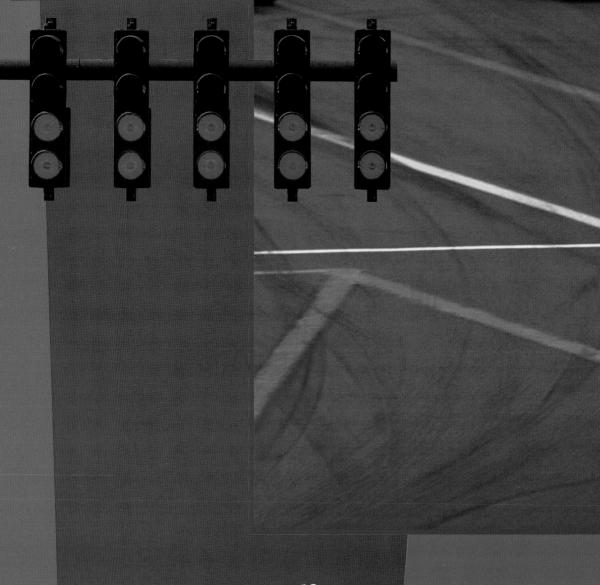

The lights are green.
Vroom!

The cars race away.
The cars go around and around the track.
Faster, faster and _faster_ they go.

The man puts up the flag.
The race is over.

The **yellow** car has
won the race!

The flag shows...

the race
is over   Yes? No?

the race has
started   Yes? No?

Some races are on roads.

The cars in the race can go
in the water, in the mud,
in the rain, and in the snow.

Racing on the road can
be very dangerous.

**Why is this kind
of racing dangerous?**

Two people are in this race car.

One person drives the car.
One person reads the map.

They have helmets to keep them safe.

The helmets keep...

the rain off   Yes? No?

the drivers safe   Yes? No?

helmet

Vroom!
Look at this car!

This car is going so *fast*, it is not on the road!

The car will...

come down	Yes? No?
crash	Yes? No?
fly away	Yes? No?

Here are more race cars.

The cars race only on a race track.

They have big wheels at the back.
They have little wheels at the front.

Look at the parachute!

The cars go so *fast* they have
a parachute to help them stop!

Index

parachute

A yes/no chart

Some race cars have parachutes to help them stop. Yes? No?

Some car races go through water and mud. Yes? No?

Race car drivers wear gloves to keep their hands warm. Yes? No?

Race cars go slowly. Yes? No?

Race car drivers wear helmets to keep their heads safe. Yes? No?

A black and white flag is waved at the end of a race. Yes? No?

Word Bank

ambulance

map

clothes

mask

flag

parachute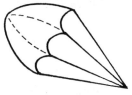

gloves

road

helmet

wheels